Airplanes

Byron Barton

Thomas Y. Crowell   New York

Copyright © 1986 by Byron Barton. Printed in Italy. All rights reserved. First Edition
Library of Congress Cataloging-in-Publication Data   Barton, Byron. Airplanes. Summary: Brief text
and illustrations present a variety of airplanes and what they do.   1. Airplanes—Juvenile literature.
[1. Airplanes] I. Title. TL547.B376 1986   387.7'334   [E]   85-47899 ISBN 0-694-00060-4
690-04532-8 (lib. bdg.)

In the sky

airplanes are flying.

This is a jet plane

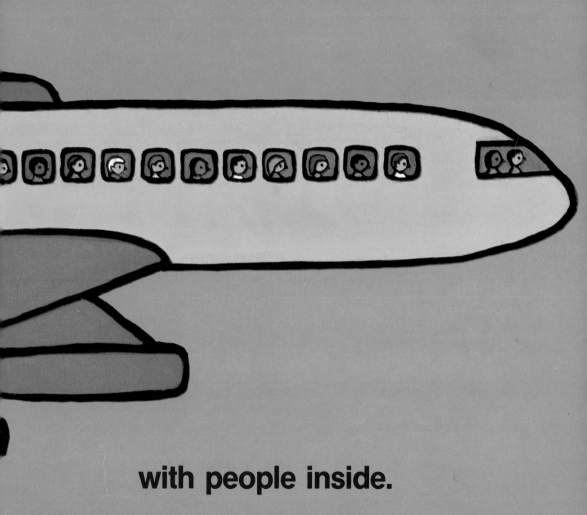

with people inside.

Here is a seaplane

landing on water.

There is an airplane

dusting the crops.

drink

There is an airplane

writing a message.

Here is a helicopter

over the city.

This is a cargo plane

loading trucks.

Here is the jet

coming in for a landing.

Here are the passengers

leaving the plane.

These are workers

cleaning and checking.

Here is a truck

loading supplies.

Here are the people

getting on board.

There is the control tower.

Get ready for takeoff.

Here is the jet plane

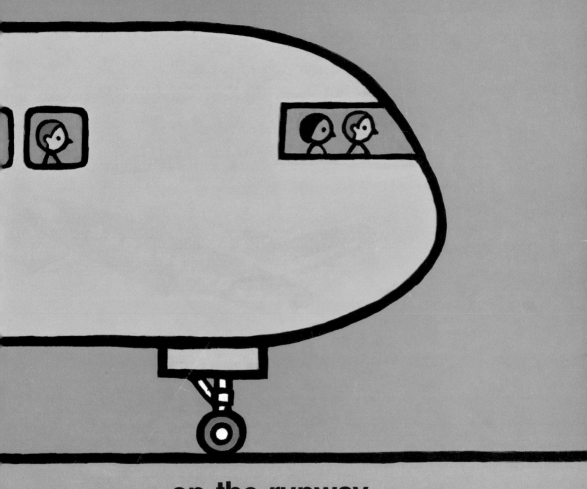

on the runway.

There goes the jet plane into the sky.